Science Essentials

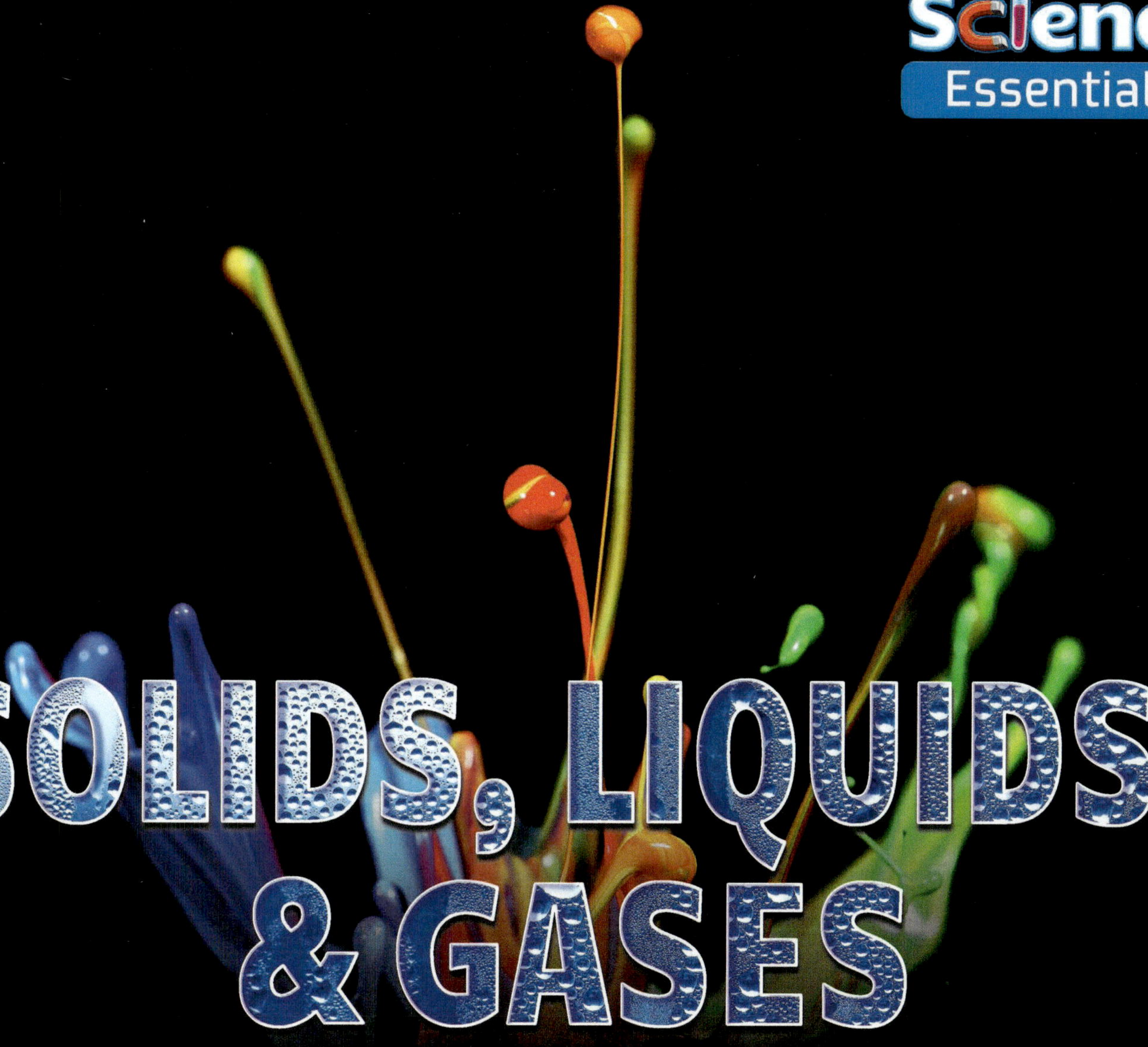

SOLIDS, LIQUIDS, & GASES

Let's Investigate

by Ruth Owen and Victoria Dobney

Consultant:

Nicky Waller

Ruby Tuesday Books

Published in 2021 by Ruby Tuesday Books Ltd.

Designer: Emma Randall
Editor: Mark J. Sachner
Production: John Lingham

Photo credits:

Alamy: 29 (center); Getty Images: 24 (bottom); Shutterstock: Cover, 1, 2—3, 4—5, 6—7, 8—9, 10—11, 12—13, 14—15, 16—17, 18—19, 20—21, 22—23, 24 (top), 24 (center), 25, 26—27, 28, 29 (bottom); Superstock: 29 (top).

Library of Congress Control Number: 2020946824
Print (hardback) ISBN 978-1-78856-192-1
Print (paperback) ISBN 978-1-78856-193-8
eBook ISBN 978-1-78856-194-5

Printed and published in the United States of America

For further information including rights and permissions requests, please contact: shan@rubytuesdaybooks.com

www.rubytuesdaybooks.com

Contents

The download button shows there are free worksheets or other resources available. Go to:
www.rubytuesdaybooks.com

Three States of Matter

If you're sitting on a chair right now, you're sitting on a solid. This book is a solid, too. If you've got a glass or bottle of water, they are also solids. And the water inside them—that's a liquid.

Take a deep breath.
You've just breathed in some **oxygen** from the air. Oxygen is a type of **gas**.

And PHWOAR! Who did that?

Yep . . . You can't see it. But that stinky smell floating through the air is another kind of gas.

Everything around us is made of **matter**.
The three main states of matter are:

Solid **Liquid** **Gas**

Solids, liquids, and gases have lots of different **properties**. A property is a quality that helps describe what an object or substance is like.

Solids

A solid can hold its shape, and it can be held in your hand.

Liquids

A liquid flows and can be poured.

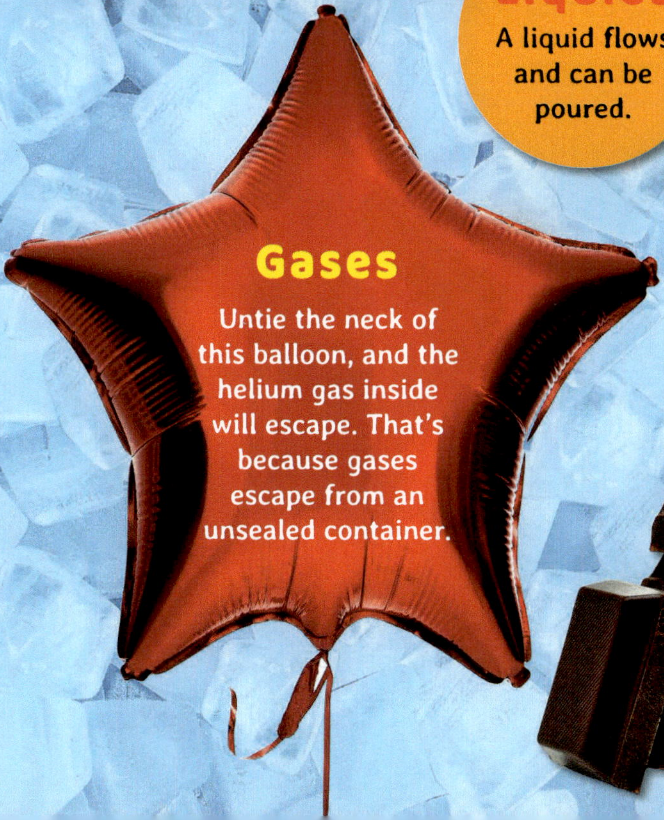

Gases

Untie the neck of this balloon, and the helium gas inside will escape. That's because gases escape from an unsealed container.

Let's Investigate

Look at each of the pictures and describe what you observe.

Are the labeled substances solids, liquids, or gases?

You will find out the answers later in the book.

What Is a Solid?

A solid is something that holds its shape and can be held. It does not flow like a liquid, but stays in one place.

A solid doesn't spread out like a gas, but always takes up the same amount of space. A solid can also be cut into smaller pieces.

A diamond in rock

Cutting pavement with a diamond blade

Cutting with Diamonds

Diamonds are gemstones that are found in rocks. They are one of the hardest solid materials we know of. Diamonds are so hard they are used to make cutting tools that can cut through other solids such as rock, metal, glass, and concrete.

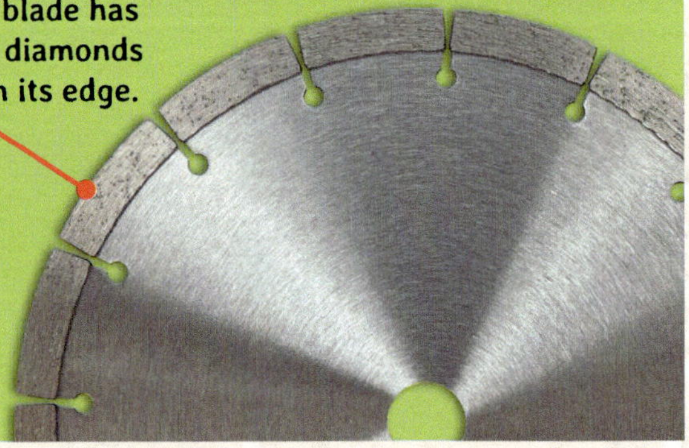

A diamond blade has tiny bits of diamonds attached on its edge.

Sand Is a Solid

If sand is a solid, why does a handful of sand pour like a liquid? Look up close, and you'll see that a handful of sand is actually made up of thousands of tiny solid pieces of rock. Together they seem to pour, but each individual grain of sand holds its shape and always takes up the same amount of space.

All matter is made up of tiny pieces called **atoms.** Atoms bond, or join together, to make **molecules.** All solids are made up of molecules. The molecules in a solid are tightly packed together. This is what helps a solid keep its shape.

This image shows how the molecules in a solid might look.

Let's Investigate

Find these everyday objects and examine them (or observe these pictures). Then try to answer the questions.

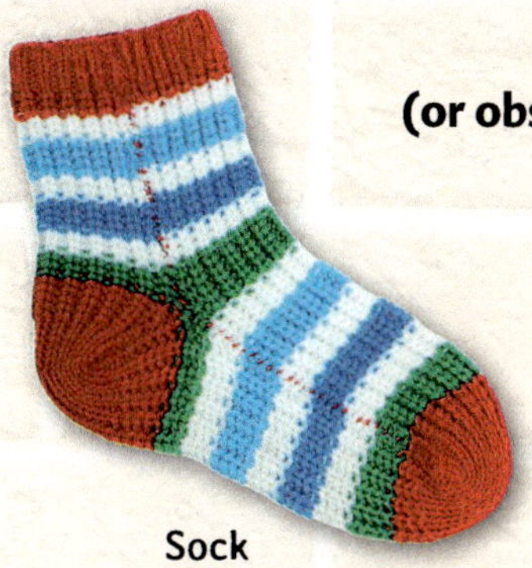

Sock

Saucepan

Shoes

Lego pieces

Lunchbox

What materials is each of the objects made of? What are the properties of the materials? Why do these properties make a material right for the job?

Properties Words

These are just some of the words that can be used to describe the properties of a solid. Can you think of some more?

hard/soft
shiny/dull
rough/smooth
opaque/transparent
translucent
stretchy/not stretchy
flexible/rigid
waterproof/not waterproof
absorbent/ not absorbent
bouncy/not bouncy

What Is a Liquid?

A liquid is a substance that pours and flows. Water, milk, and orange juice are all liquids.

Unlike a solid, a liquid is difficult to hold.

Liquids don't have a shape. They take the shape of the containers they are in—for example, a liquid will take the shape of a bottle, bathtub, and even an elephant's trunk!

When a liquid changes its shape, its **volume** stays the same. A quart of orange juice in a pitcher is still a quart when it's poured into different glasses—even though its shape has changed.

Wonderful H_2O

There is more water on Earth than any other type of liquid.

People sometimes call water H_2O. This is because it is made up of atoms of **hydrogen** (H) and oxygen (O). The atoms bond together to make water molecules.

A water molecule is made of two hydrogen atoms and one oxygen atom—H_2O.

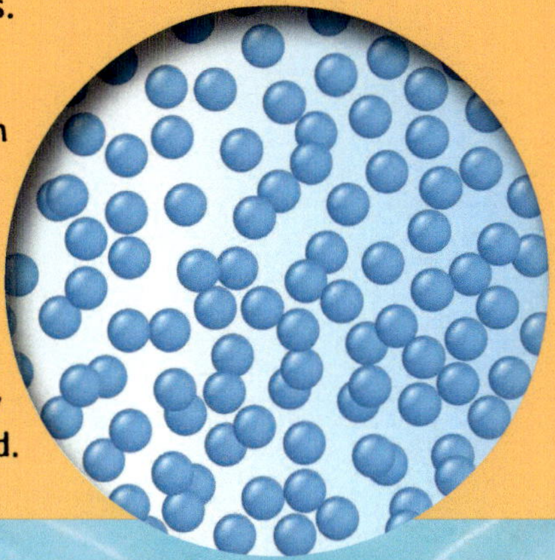

The molecules in a liquid are not as tightly packed as in a solid.

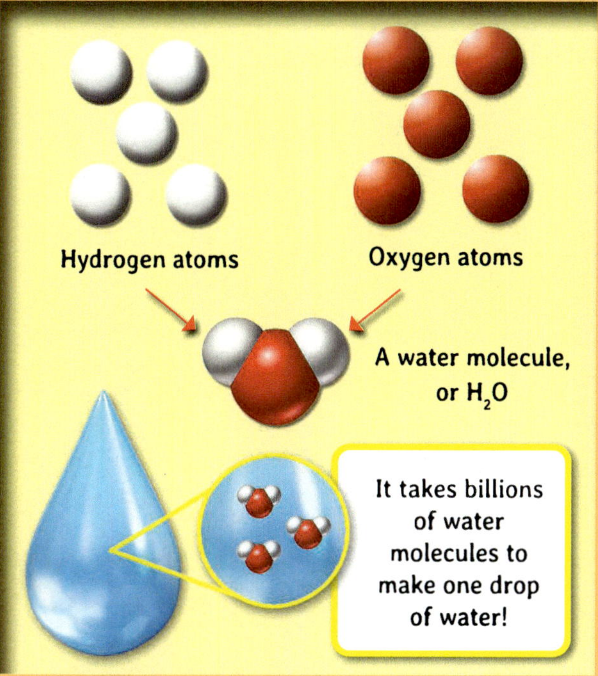

Let's Investigate

Liquids can be thick or thin. The thickness of a liquid and how quickly or slowly it flows is called its **viscosity**. Water flows quickly and has a low viscosity. Honey flows slowly and has a high viscosity.

Think about these everyday liquids. Do they have a low, medium, or high viscosity?

Chocolate milk

Ketchup

Dishwashing liquid

Cooking oil

Paint

Pancake batter

Tea

What Is a Gas?

There are gases all around us, but because most are invisible, we mostly can't see them.

Gases do not have a fixed shape. They spread out and change their volume to fill up a container. When gas escapes from a container, it spreads throughout the whole room.

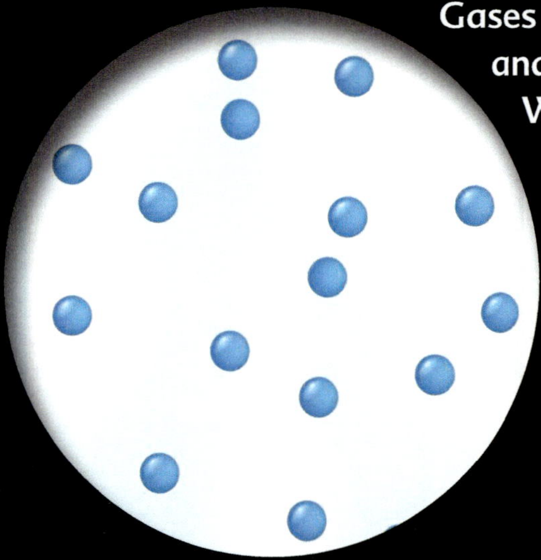

The molecules in a gas are much farther apart than in a liquid or solid.

Making Fizzy Drinks Fizzy

Gases can be compressed or squashed. Fizzy soda is made by compressing lots of carbon dioxide into a flavored liquid inside a bottle or other container. Being compressed makes the gas **dissolve** and become part of the liquid. But when you unscrew the top of the bottle . . . PHISSSSHHHH! As the pressure in the bottle decreases, the carbon dioxide instantly becomes a gas again. The gas creates bubbles in the drink and starts to escape into the air.

Once all the gas has escaped, your soda will be flat.

Excuse Me!

If you burp after swallowing some soda, it's because the bubbles of gas are now inside you and are trying to escape!

⚠ WARNING

Don't ever try touching steam from a kettle because it is very hot and can seriously burn you.

Making Steam

If you said that the steam from the kettle on page 5 is a gas, you were correct. But the steam isn't actually the white cloud that we see in the air. When water is heated, it changes from a liquid into an invisible gas called **water vapor**. This gas escapes from the kettle's spout. Once the water vapor starts floating in the air, it cools down. Then it changes back into water. The white cloud is actually tiny, tiny drops of liquid water.

Let's Talk!

Your body is made up of all three states of matter. What solids, liquids, and gases make up you?

(The answer is on page 32.)

The Air We Breathe

Unless we are underwater in a swimming pool or bathtub, we are always surrounded by air. So what is air made of?

Air is made up of a mixture of different gases, including nitrogen, oxygen, carbon dioxide, argon and water vapor. Molecules of these gases float around us, and we breathe them in and out.

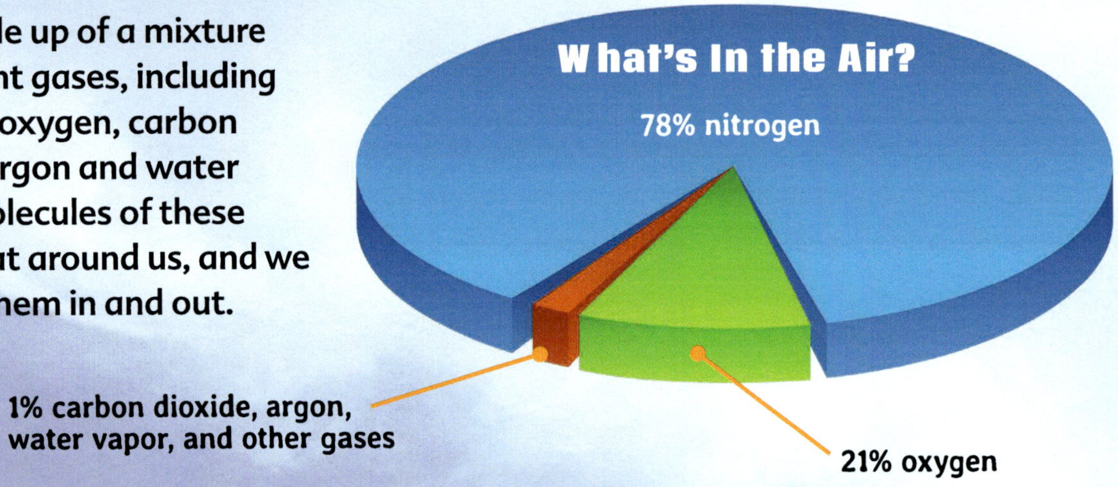

Air also contains bits of dust and dirt. Most of these **particles** are too small for us to see without a **microscope**.

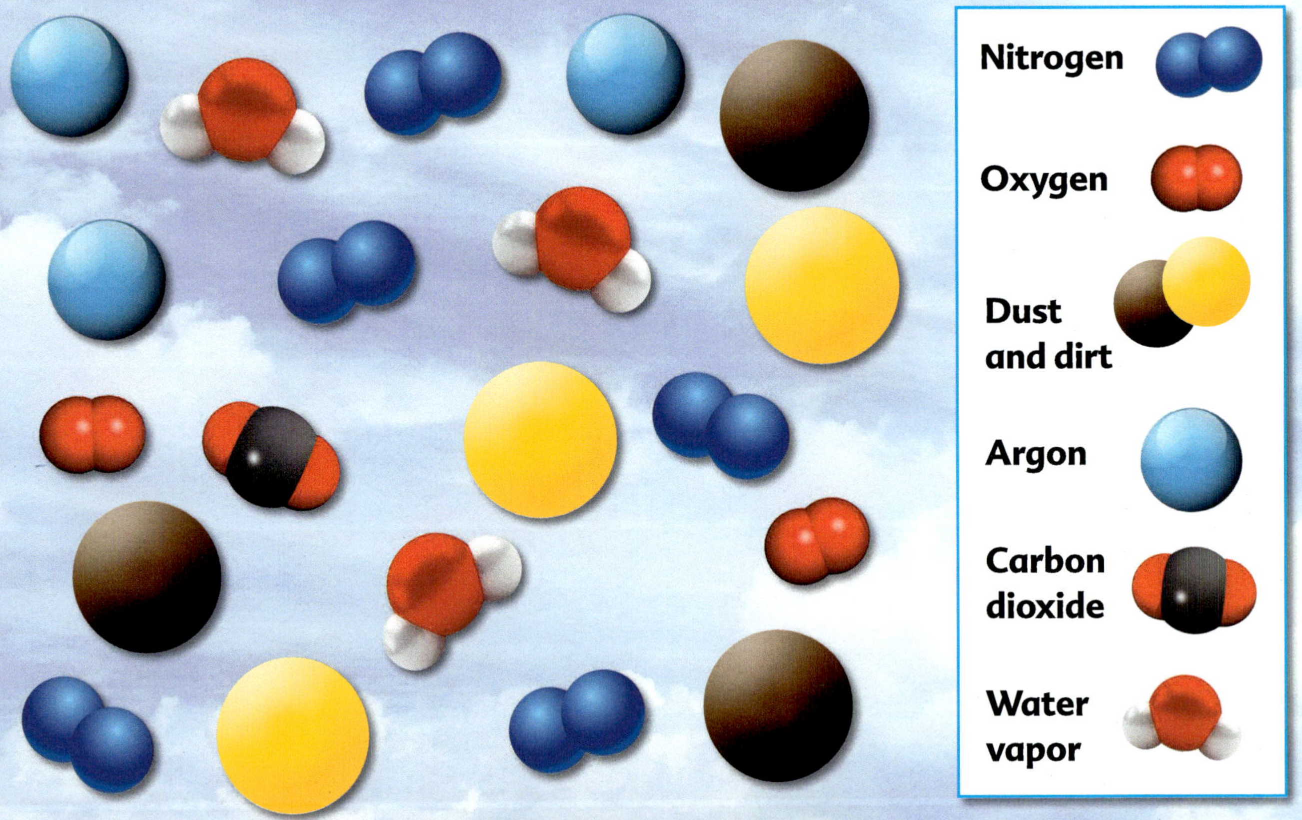

Let's Test It

We don't usually notice or feel the air around us. But try fanning your face with this book. The cool breeze you feel is air being moved back and forth by the book's movements.

Smells Good!

That delicious barbecue aroma . . . the smell of freshly cut grass . . . what exactly are smells? When food is cooked, gases are released that float through the air and into your nose. It's the same when grass is mowed. The grass releases chemicals that float off in all directions as gases. When we smell something nice or nasty, it's because that object or substance is giving off gases that our noses can detect.

Let's Investigate

If you make a bowl shape with your hands, you will be holding some air. You can't see the air, though, or feel that it's there. So does air actually weigh anything? Let's investigate.

Equipment:
- 3 pieces of string, each about 20 inches (50 cm) long
- A ruler
- 2 balloons
- A pin
- A notebook and pen

Does air have weight?

Method:

1. Tie one piece of string around the center of the ruler.
2. Blow up two balloons so they are the same size and tie each with a knot.
3. Tie a piece of string around each balloon's knot and then tie one balloon to each end of the ruler.

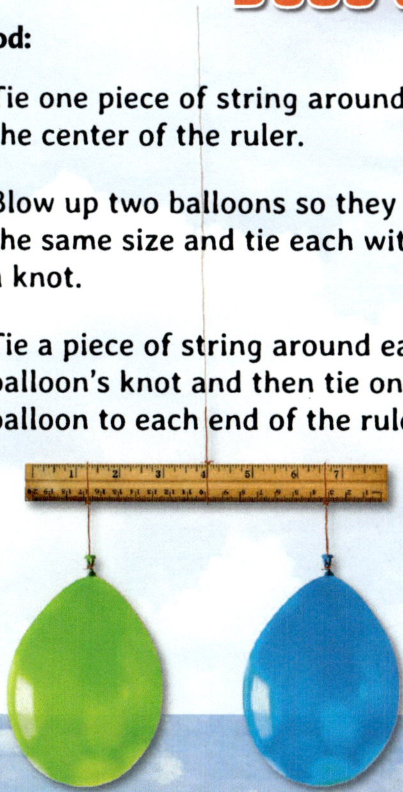

4. Adjust the three strings as needed so the balloons are level and balanced like a set of scales.

What do you think will happen if you pop one of the balloons?

5. Write your prediction in your notebook and then pop a balloon.

What do you observe happened?
Do the results match your prediction?
Does air have weight? Explain your conclusion.

(There are some answers on page 32.)

The Water Cycle

Water can exist as a liquid, a gas, and a solid. The way in which water changes from one state to another is called the water cycle.

How does it work?

The Story of a Puddle

The rain has stopped, leaving behind a puddle. The Sun comes out and starts to warm the rainwater. As the Sun gets hotter, the puddle gets smaller and smaller.

Soon the puddle has dried up and is gone, but the water hasn't disappeared. It has **evaporated** and is now floating in the air as a gas called water vapor.

The water vapor floats up . . .

. . . 1 mile (1.5 km) above the ground . . .

. . . 2 miles (3 km) above the ground . . .

. . . up and up it goes.

When a liquid is heated and turns into a gas, the process is called **evaporation**.

When a gas is cooled down and turns into a liquid, the process is called condensation.

High in the sky, the air is colder than on Earth. The vapor starts to cool down. As it does, the gas **condenses** and changes back into tiny droplets of liquid water.

The very tiny droplets of water stick to particles of dust. They join up with many other droplets and form a cloud. The wind blows the cloud many miles from the place where the puddle was on the ground.

Each droplet in the cloud is smaller than the period at the end of this sentence. They start to stick together to form raindrops.

The raindrops grow bigger . . .

. . . and bigger . . .

. . . and bigger.

Let's Test It

Is there water vapor in the air inside your home or classroom?

Stand two dry glasses on a table or countertop. Put five ice cubes in one glass. Wait for 15 minutes.

What do you observe? How do you explain what has happened?

(There are some answers on page 32.)

The Water Cycle:

Around and Around

The raindrops in the cloud grow bigger and heavier. Finally, they are too heavy to stay up in the sky any longer.

The water that was in the puddle just a few weeks ago comes pouring back down to Earth as rain.

Making Snow

If the air around a cloud is very cold, water droplets may freeze and become tiny solid crystals of ice. The crystals join together to form snowflakes. Then they fall back to Earth as snow.

Up to 200 crystals might stick together to make one snowflake.

Let's Talk!

How might a snowman become a liquid and a gas?

The rain might land in the ocean, quickly evaporate, and become water vapor again. Or it may stay as salty seawater for tens, hundreds, or thousands of years.

Prehistoric Water

All the water on Earth has been here since the planet first formed. It has been going around and around the water cycle for billions of years. In fact, the next time you take a shower, you might be washing in recycled water that was once part of a stream where dinosaurs came to drink!

The rain could land in a stream, river, or lake. It might fall on a mountaintop, freeze, and become ice. It might even splash to the ground, form a new puddle, and soon become rain or snow again.

This process is called the water cycle. Everywhere on Earth, water is moving through the different stages of the water cycle . . .

. . . over and over . . .

. . . and over again.

The Water Cycle

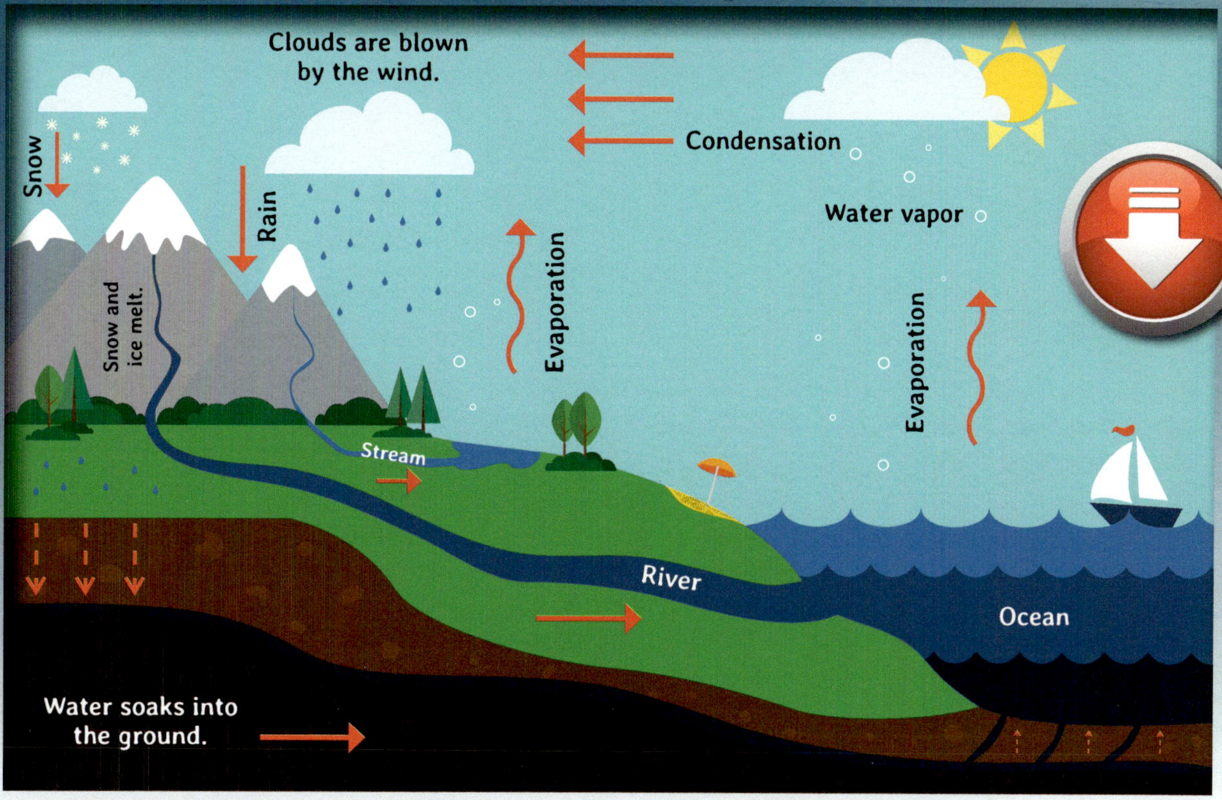

Can you describe the ways in which water is moving through the water cycle in this diagram?

Heating, Melting, Cooling, Freezing

Liquids can be changed into solids, and some solids can be changed into liquids. This is done by cooling or heating them. Let's Investigate!

When water (liquid) is cooled to a temperature of 32°F (0°C), it changes to ice (solid). This change is called freezing. It's not just water that can be frozen. Other liquids can freeze, too.

An Expanding Solid

Once water becomes a solid, you might expect its molecules to be closer together like other solids. But ice doesn't act like other solids. As water freezes, its molecules actually move farther apart. This makes the ice expand, so it takes up more space than liquid water.

Let's Investigate

How quickly do liquids become solids?

Equipment:
- An ice cube tray
- Your choice of liquids for testing—for example: water, milk, honey, cooking oil, chocolate sauce, ketchup, dishwashing soap, shower gel
- Some small spoons
- A freezer
- A clock or phone for timing
- A notebook and pen

Method:

1. Carefully squeeze or spoon a different liquid into each section of the ice cube tray.

How quickly do you think the water will freeze? How about the other liquids? Do you think any of the liquids won't freeze? Why do you think this?

2. Write your predictions in your notebook. Put the ice cube tray in the freezer and start your timer.
3. Check the tray after 30 minutes. Carefully observe the liquids and record your observations.
4. Decide when to check again and repeat step 3. Keep checking and recording.

Did any of your results match your predictions?

(There is some further information on page 32.)

When ice (solid) is heated, it changes to water (liquid). This change is called melting. Some other solids can also be melted and turned into liquids by heating them.

When temperatures rise above 32°F (0°C), ice starts to melt. What temperature does this thermometer show?

Let's Investigate

Can hot water turn a solid to a liquid?

Equipment:

- 6 substances for testing—for example: a square of chocolate, a cube of butter, a cube of hard cheese, a cube of soap, a piece of crayon, an ice cube
- 6 small foil dishes
- A large baking sheet with raised sides
- A notebook and pen
- An adult helper
- A thermometer

Method:

1. You are going to use very hot water to try to melt the solids. Carefully examine each one.

Which of these solids do you think will melt?

2. Place each solid in a foil dish and then put the six foil dishes inside the baking sheet.
3. Now ask your adult helper to carefully pour hot water from a kettle into the sheet. DO NOT TOUCH THE WATER. Ask your helper to hold the thermometer in the water and then show you. Read the temperature and record it in your notebook.
4. Carefully observe what happens. Record your results by writing a statement that describes what happened to each substance.
5. ALLOW THE WATER TO COOL DOWN before putting away your materials. You could try this investigation again by putting the six substances outside in the sun on a hot day.

Does It Dissolve?

Take a glass of water and stir a teaspoon of salt into the liquid. At first the water looks a little cloudy, but gradually the water goes back to being transparent, or see-through. Has the salt disappeared?

Even if you can't see salt in water, you can prove it's there by taking a tiny sip.

No! The salt is still there but it has dissolved, or mixed with the water.

A mixture of water and a dissolved substance is called a **solution.**

Substances that dissolve in water are called **soluble** substances. Substances that do not dissolve are **insoluble** substances.

This image shows grains of salt viewed with a microscope. Each tiny solid grain forms as a crystal.

Let's Investigate

Once salt is dissolved in water, can it ever go back to being solid salt again? Let's investigate.

Equipment:
- A measuring cup
- 2 teaspoons of salt
- 3.5 ounces (100 ml) of water
- A spoon
- A dark-colored shallow dish
- A notebook and pen

Method:

1. Using the spoon, mix the salt and water together in the cup until the salt dissolves and the water is transparent.
2. Pour the water into the shallow dish. Place the dish in a warm, sunny place such as on a windowsill.

What do you think will happen to the water? Write your prediction in your notebook.

3. Keep checking the dish over the next few days. Observe what happens and record your results. Complete your experiment by writing down your conclusion.

What happened to the water? What happened to the salt? Can you explain why this happened?

Let's Investigate

Try testing some everyday substances to discover if they will dissolve in water.

Tea

Crushed chalk

Instant coffee

Pepper

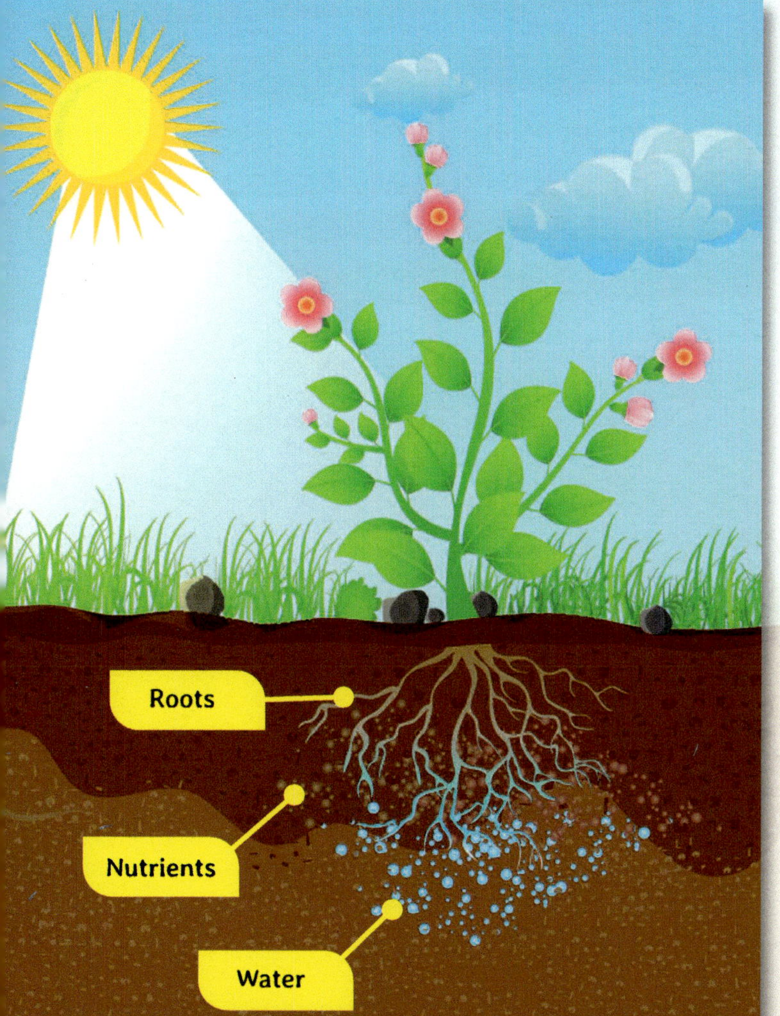

The Perfect Solution

Water is able to dissolve more substances than any other liquid. This property of water is very important for plants. Plants need substances called **nutrients** to help them grow and be healthy. Nutrients are found in the soil. They dissolve in water, and then plants take in the nutritious watery solutions through their roots.

Is it Soluble or Insoluble?

Equipment:

- Substances for testing—for example: sugar, instant coffee, tea (from a tea bag), sand, pepper, crushed chalk, flour
- Small clear plastic cups or containers (check the recycling)
- A pitcher of cold water
- A teaspoon
- Paper towel for wiping the spoon
- A notebook and pen

Method:

1. Carefully examine the substances.

What do you think will happen when you mix each substance with water?
- ***It will dissolve.***
- ***It will float and won't dissolve.***
- ***It will sink to the bottom and won't dissolve.***

2. Record your predictions in your notebook.
3. Fill a cup or container with water and stir in a teaspoon of one of the substances. Observe what happens.
4. Record your results and then test the next substance in a different cup.

Which substances were soluble, and which were insoluble? Do your results match your predictions?

Can you tell by feeling a substance if it will be soluble or insoluble?

Can Salty Seawater Become a Solid?

About 97 percent of the water on Earth is saltwater. But where does the salt come from, and can salty seawater freeze?

Seawater is salty because tiny particles of salt have dissolved in the water.

Many types of rocks contain particles of salt. When waves crash against rocky cliffs, tiny pieces of rock and salt get washed into the sea.

A quart (1 liter) of seawater contains about two teaspoons of salt.

When it rains on land, rainwater wears away mountains and other rocks. The rock crumbles and gets carried by the rain into streams and rivers. Then the rivers carry tiny bits of rock and salt into the sea.

Earth's Freshwater

Just 3 percent of Earth's water is **freshwater**. Most of this water is frozen in **glaciers**, on mountains, and in Antarctica and the Arctic. The rest is in streams, rivers, ponds, lakes, and under the ground as **groundwater**.

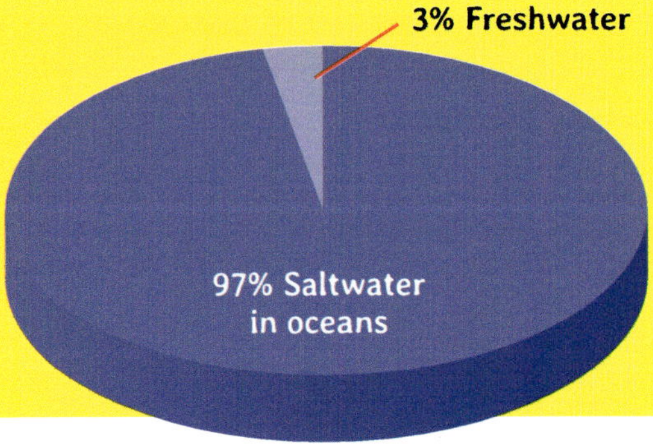

Little by Little

All over the world, thousands of rivers flow into the oceans. The water in every river contains some salt, so the amount of salt in the sea builds up.

Freshwater freezes and turns to solid ice when its temperature drops to 32°F (0°C).

Seawater doesn't freeze until its temperature drops to about 28°F (-2°C). That's because it contains salt.

In some very cold parts of the world, the surface of the ocean does freeze. But most of Earth's oceans stay liquid all the time.

Frozen seawater in the Arctic

Ice is lighter than liquid water, so it floats on the surface.

Let's Investigate

If salt makes it harder for water to freeze, can salt also melt ice? Let's test salt against some other substances.

Equipment:

- A tablespoon of salt
- A tablespoon of sand
- A tablespoon of sugar
- 12 ice cubes (of the same size)
- 4 small bowls
- A clock or phone for timing
- A notebook and pen

Method:

1. Put three ice cubes in each bowl.
2. Quickly sprinkle the salt over one bowl of ice cubes. Sprinkle the sand over a second bowl and sugar over a third. The fourth bowl will just contain ice cubes. Place the bowls in a refrigerator.

Which bowl of ice cubes do you think will melt first? How about last?

3. Predict the order in which the ice cubes will melt and record this in your notebook. Check the ice cubes every 20 minutes for an hour.

Which substance melted ice the fastest? Did your results match the order in your predictions? Can you think of a way that your discovery could be helpful in everyday life?

(The answer is on page 32.)

Mixed-Up Mixtures

Scientists often have to separate solutions or mixtures of different substances so they can study the individual ingredients. There are lots of ways to do this.

To separate a solution, the water can be evaporated. For example, if saltwater is boiled, the water heats up and evaporates, leaving the solid salt behind.

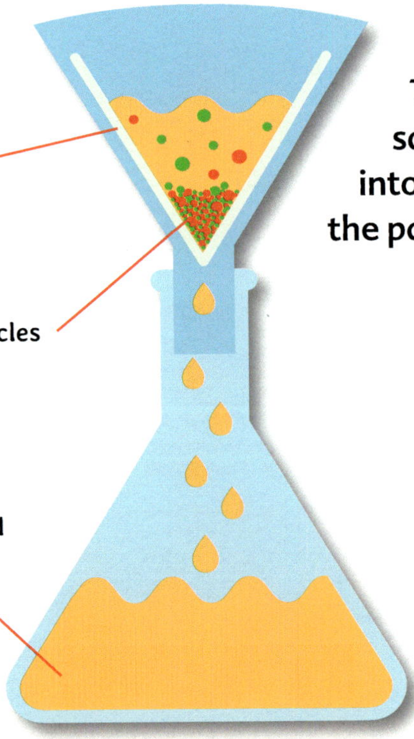

To separate an insoluble substance such as sand from water, the mixture can be filtered into a container through filter paper. Tiny holes in the paper let the water through but trap the sand.

Pete Ceglinski empties a filter called a catch bag from a Seabin.

The catch bag can trap tiny particles of plastic that are smaller than a grain of rice.

Separating Trash from Seawater

Australian surfers Andrew Turton and Pete Ceglinski invented a floating waste container called the Seabin that filters trash from the water in ports and marinas. As the Seabin floats at the surface, a pump sucks the seawater into the container along with plastic bags, bottles, disposable coffee cups, and other trash. Then the water is pumped out, and the trash stays trapped in the "catch bag." The Seabin even has sponge-like pads to soak up oil, spilled fuel from boats, and other chemicals.

To separate particles of different sizes, sieves and strainers can be used.

This sieve would trap marble-sized objects but let through smaller pea-sized particles, grains of sand, or water.

Let's Investigate

Separation Challenge

Test your problem-solving skills by challenging a friend to a separation challenge!

Method:

1. Make a mixture of insoluble substances for your friend to separate. Choose 10 ingredients from the list or think of your own.
2. Fill a jar with water, add the ingredients, and mix them thoroughly. Your friend must do the same. Now swap jars.
3. You must not put your hands in the jars or touch the water or ingredients at any time. But you can use any items from the equipment list (and ideas of your own) to help you separate your mixture.
4. As every part of an ingredient is removed from the water, place that ingredient on your sheet of paper.
5. The winner is the scientist who is able to completely remove the most ingredients from their jar. If you are both able to remove all 10, the first person to complete the task wins the challenge!

When you've finished the task, carefully pour out your water, but don't let any pieces of plastic or other objects go down the drain.

Equipment:
- Your choice of insoluble substances from the list below
- 2 large jars
- Water
- 2 spoons with long handles
- 2 sheets of printer paper
- Straining spoon, coffee filters, sieve, tea strainer, magnet, paper towel, bowls, pitchers

Ingredients List:
- Lego pieces
- Paper clips
- Beads
- Marbles
- Cake sprinkles
- Cooking oil
- Sand
- Pepper
- Potting compost
- Gravel
- Dry rice
- Cornflakes
- Crushed chalk
- Flour
- Filter coffee
- Raisins
- Coins
- Small metal screws
- Popcorn
- Grass trimmings

No Going Back!

When water changes and freezes into ice, this is a reversible change. What does that mean?

A reversible change is one that can be undone, or reversed. Ice can be heated so it melts and goes back to being water.

Sometimes, however, substances change, and they can't easily go back. These changes are called **irreversible** changes.

Frying an egg is an irreversible change. The cooked egg can't go back to being raw!

Let's Talk!

These cupcakes were made by melting solid chocolate. Then the hot liquid chocolate was mixed with syrup, butter, and Rice Krispies. Finally, the liquid chocolate cooled and became solid again, binding all the ingredients together.

Do you think that making these cupcakes is a reversible change or an irreversible change?

(The answer is on page 32.)

Irreversible Changes: Rust

Rusting is an irreversible change that happens to some metals. Rust is a crumbly, orange-brown substance. It forms when iron, or metals that contain iron, get wet. The oxygen in the water creates a **chemical reaction** with the iron. Once rust starts to form, it corrodes, or eats into the metal, making holes and weakening it. Rusty metal crumbles into flaky orange dust. It can never go back to being hard, strong, and shiny.

Changing Wood into Charcoal

When a fire burns, it usually uses lots of oxygen. But when people make charcoal, they enclose the wood in a sealed container to keep oxygen from getting to the wood. This makes the wood burn more slowly. Any water in the wood evaporates as water vapor. Other substances also evaporate and turn to gases. The wood gets drier and drier and starts to blacken. Finally, the wood has gone through an irreversible change to become charcoal.

Wood

Charcoal

Charcoal is used as a fuel for barbecues and as a material for drawing.

Melting Metals for Recycling

Aluminum is a metal that is used to make drink cans, foil, and parts for cars and planes. It's difficult to imagine strong, solid metal becoming a liquid. However, aluminum can be melted and recycled over and over again.

Once aluminum cans are collected from your home, they are crushed and delivered to a recycling plant in large bales. Next, the cans are shredded.

Each bale weighs about 2,200 pounds (1,000 kg) and contains around 65,000 cans.

The shredded, scrap aluminum is heated in a process called decoating. This process creates a chemical reaction that removes the paint and turns it into gases.

Shredded, decoated scrap aluminum

Metal from Rock

Aluminum is found in a type of rock called bauxite. The rock goes through many different processes using heat and chemicals to break it down so the metal can be extracted, or removed.

The shredded aluminum is heated in a giant, oven-like furnace. It is so hot inside, the solid metal melts and becomes a scorching liquid.

The temperature inside the furnace is 1,346°F (730°C).

The liquid metal is poured into a giant mold where it cools, hardens, and becomes a solid block called an ingot.

A 65-foot- (10-m-) long ingot contains the metal from 1.5 million recycled cans.

The ingots are taken on a truck to a factory called a rolling mill. Here they are heated to soften them again. Then they are passed back and forth through giant rollers—just like rolling pastry.

Each ingot becomes a roll of newly made aluminum that is ready to go to a factory to be made into more cans and other products.

The roll is 6 miles (10 km) long.

The aluminum on the roll is as thin as paper.

Glossary

atoms
Tiny particles that make up everything around us.

chemical reaction
A change that takes place between two or more substances and creates something new.

condensation
The process during which a gas cools down and changes into a liquid. For example, water vapor (gas) condenses and becomes water (liquid).

condense
To change from a gas to a liquid.

crystal
A substance (such as the mineral salt) that has formed in a shape with straight edges and smooth sides, or faces.

dissolve
To become mixed into a liquid.

evaporate
To change from a liquid to a gas.

evaporation
The process during which a liquid heats up and changes into a gas. For example, water (liquid) evaporates and becomes water vapor (gas).

freshwater
Water that does not contain salt.

gas
A state of matter. Gases float in air and are neither solids nor liquids. Most gases, such as oxygen, are invisible.

glacier
A huge mass of ice, often up to 100 feet (30 m) thick, that moves very slowly over an area of land.

groundwater
Water that has soaked into the ground and collected in the soil or between rocks.

hydrogen
A colorless gas with no smell.

insoluble
Not able to dissolve in a liquid.

irreversible
Not able to be reversed or undone.

liquid
A state of matter. Liquids flow and do not have a shape. Water and milk are both liquids.

matter
All the real, 3D stuff around us (blood, bones, water, air, metal, rock, chocolate, books, plastic bottles) and the substances and materials from which it is made. The three main states of matter are solid, liquid, and gas.

microscope
An instrument used to see things that are too small to be seen with the eyes alone.

molecule
A group of atoms that are bonded together. For example, a water molecule (H_2O) is made of two hydrogen atoms and one oxygen atom.

nutrients
Substances needed by a plant or animal to help it live and grow. For example, nitrogen is a nutrient that helps plants grow healthy leaves.

oxygen
A gas in the air that has no color and no smell. Oxygen is produced by plants. People and animals breathe oxygen.

particles
Tiny parts of something.

property
A quality that helps describe what an object or substance is like—for example, shiny or dull, rough or smooth.

reversible
Able to be reversed or undone. For example, freezing water is a change that can be reversed.

solid
A state of matter. Solids hold their shape and can be held and cut. Wood and metal are both solids.

soluble
Able to dissolve in a liquid.

solution
A mixture of a liquid and a dissolved substance. For example, saltwater is a solution.

viscosity
The thickness of a liquid.

volume
The amount of space a substance takes up. For example, the volume of a liquid might be 1 quart (1 liter) or less than half a cup (100 ml).

water cycle
The movement of water on Earth through its three states. For example, water evaporates and floats into the sky as water vapor. Then it condenses into liquid or freezes into ice, forms clouds, and falls back to Earth as rain or snow.

water vapor
The gas state of water. Water vapor rises and spreads out through the air.

Index

Answers

Page 11:
Many parts of our bodies are solids, including bones, muscles, skin, nails, eyeballs, heart, and brain. Our bodies contain liquids that include blood, saliva, urine, tears, digestive juices for breaking down our food, and tiny amounts of water inside every single cell. Gases include oxygen, carbon dioxide, nitrogen, and hydrogen sulfide, which is one of the smelly gases that builds up in your intestines and is expelled from your bottom!

Page 13:
When you popped one balloon, the other one pulled the ruler (scales) down. That's because it was heavier than the popped or empty balloon. The air inside made the balloon heavier and shows that air has weight.

Page 15:
After 15 minutes, the glass containing the ice cubes has water on the outside. The ice cubes made the glass cold. Water vapor in the air all around us touched the cold glass, cooled down, and condensed back into drops of liquid water, or condensation. The empty glass is not cold, so no condensation has formed on this glass. This is a good way to show that there is always some water vapor in the air.

Page 18:
The water probably froze first. The oil probably didn't freeze but just became thicker. All liquids have a freezing point, but oil and some other liquids freeze at a much lower temperature than the temperature inside a home freezer.

Page 23:
The ice cubes sprinkled with salt melted first. Salt makes it harder for water to freeze, and it is also able to melt ice. In winter, salt can be sprinkled on roads and pavement to melt ice and snow and make it safer to get around.

Page 26:
This change is irreversible. If you stood the cakes outside in the hot sun or close to a radiator, the chocolate would melt and become liquid. But it would be very difficult to now remove the syrup, butter, and Rice Krispies from the mixture.